MW01135380

THE MANY WORLDS OF
RORLITZER
SCREW

THE MANY WORLDS OF
RORLITZER
SCREW

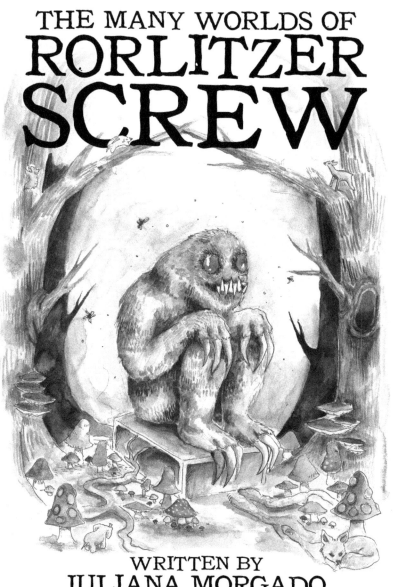

WRITTEN BY
JULIANA MORGADO
ILLUSTRATED BY LILLY SHURBET

ARCHWAY
PUBLISHING

This is a work of fiction. All of the characters, names, incidents, organizations, and dialogue in this novel are either the products of the author's imagination or are used fictitiously.

Archway Publishing books may be ordered through booksellers or by contacting:

Archway Publishing
1663 Liberty Drive
Bloomington, IN 47403
www.archwaypublishing.com
1 (888) 242-5904

Because of the dynamic nature of the Internet, any web addresses or links contained in this book may have changed since publication and may no longer be valid. The views expressed in this work are solely those of the author and do not necessarily reflect the views of the publisher, and the publisher hereby disclaims any responsibility for them.

ISBN: 978-1-4808-7500-5 (sc)
ISBN: 978-1-4808-7501-2 (e)

Library of Congress Control Number: 2019903744

Print information available on the last page.

Archway Publishing rev. date: 4/9/2019

*To my husband and his
unwavering belief in me.*

*To my parents for their commitment
to education and art.*

There's a separate world apart from ours,
where shadows are doors letting souls through,
with fields of bone instead of flowers;
this is the world of Rorlitzer Screw.

Where suns beam red instead of yellow,
they watch through cracks known by only a few.
Where timelines blend and cosmos narrow,
these are the worlds of Rorlitzer Screw.

THE MANY WORLDS OF
RORLITZER
SCREW

ONE

JUST BEFORE MIDNIGHT, ELEVEN-YEAR-old Collin awoke to the sound of rustling. He emerged from his blankets and followed the noise into the hallway. The sweater he wore to bed hung almost to his knees; the long sleeves fell far past his hands, like extra wiggling skin without muscle or bone to solidify it. In the glow of the night-light, his body made a dripping silhouette against the hardwood floors.

The noise was coming from his parents' bedroom.

He twisted the knob and pushed open the door.

"I'm sorry, sweetie—did I wake you?" Collin's mother sat in front of an open closet. Clothes and shoes surrounded her and the half-empty boxes she was in the process of filling.

"What are you doing?" Collin asked.

"I'm clearing out the closet," she said.

"But why *that* closet?"

Silence swelled between them.

Finally, Collin's mother answered, "I read that it would be good to pack away some of your father's things now. It helps to make space—"

"You're throwing them out?" Collin's voice rose in panic. Outside, an owl hooted from the nearby forest.

"No, sweetie, I'm not throwing anything out. I'm just boxing it up—putting it in the basement." She added, "It's healthy, you know?"

Collin didn't respond. His eyes wandered across the heaps of clothes, and he was struck by dueling desires to study each item intimately and also not to look at any of them at all.

"Here. I found this tucked away. I've never seen it before; I thought you might want it." She handed him a small wooden box—something of his father's from years ago. "The latch is stuck, but it feels empty. Maybe you can get it open and keep something special inside. Just don't let Kaitlin get hold of it. Antiques like this are just toys to toddlers."

Collin took the box and turned back toward the hallway. As he began to leave the bedroom, his mother added, "And, Collin, if you're going to keep wearing that sweater, let's get it in the wash, okay?"

TWO

ARMED WITH A FLASHLIGHT UNDER
the secrecy of his comforter, Collin first inspected
the outside of the wooden box. Mesmerizing filigree
swirled from every edge, like exploring tentacles from
emerging octopi. Dainty tableaus were carved onto the
sides. The latch on the front was unlike any he had ever
seen.

As he tilted the box to observe all sides, he heard a
rattle and felt the distinct weighted shift of items
toppling from within.
There was something
inside after all.

Metal hinges held
the box together in
the back, and though
the clasp on the front

3

appeared delicate, it wouldn't budge. *Maybe I should just leave it shut,* Collin thought. But then he considered the contents inside—whatever it was or whatever they were had once belonged to his father. He had put them in there; he had stowed them away. Not even Collin's mother was privy to this secret. Collin decided that was a part of his father's life he desperately wanted to share.

He wedged his finger farther beneath the latch. The tight force pinched his fingertip a painful bright white until finally it unlocked. Collin slowly opened the lid.

Inside he found three golden animals, none bigger than two inches tall: a tiger, a rhinoceros, and a giraffe. One by one, he examined the animals until he held the miniature zoo in the palm of his hand. There was surprising weight to them, as if ten dollars' worth of quarters were melted down into three-dimensional animal crackers. *I've never seen anything like them,* he thought.

The minuscule details on each were unbelievable. Whiskers around the tiger's mouth were specifically defined and distinct from its already striped face. Metal fluffs of fur topped the horns of the giraffe. Leather texture was carved into the rhino's hide, displaying its coarse and protective skin. The craftsmanship was obvious, even to Collin, who gazed at their twinkling metal bodies in the focused beams of a flashlight.

Then, with careful, slow hands, he repacked the beautiful menagerie from his father. With all the animals back in the box, he shut the lid and slid it onto his nightstand. He clicked off the flashlight, curled beneath his covers, and fell back asleep.

THREE

JUST AFTER THREE, A LOUD CRASH awoke Collin from his dreamscape. He was startled and instantly sat upright, his eyes straining through the darkness. This time the noise had come from within his room.

Then he saw it: near his bedside, the wooden box had toppled from his nightstand and lay open and empty on the floor below. He leaped out of bed, and on all fours, he searched for his tiny animals.

But they weren't near the box.

Or under his bed.

Or blending in with the pattern of his rug.

They weren't anywhere.

Collin's eyes filled with tears. As he sat on the floor, the quiet of the night was disturbed only by the heavy, sputtered breathing of him trying not to cry. How many decades had his father held on to these? And now Collin had lost them in the span of one night. *What could have pushed it off?* he thought. *The latch! I know I shut the latch!*

But there was another sound too. A scratching? A tapping?

Collin stood from the floor to follow the sound. He walked to his window, left partially open so he could feel the autumn-night breeze as he slept. He peeked through the blinds and saw a branch from the front yard sycamore scraping against the glass. In a row across the branch walked three tiny golden animals.

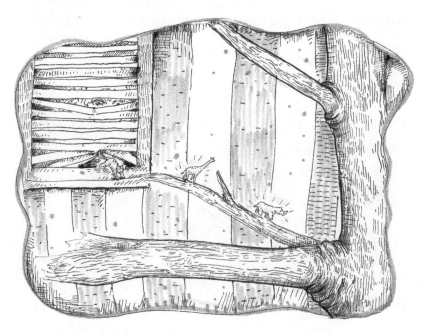

With wide eyes, Collin watched them crisscross down the limbs of the tree. They made it all the way to the trunk before he thought to follow them. He opened the window wide enough to fit through and lunged.

His arms wrapped around the first branches they touched, and gravity assisted his body in clambering to the ground. He landed with a thud but stood and peered through the darkness until he found the animals walking through the grass, headed toward the tree line. *They're so fast,* he thought. *Where could they be going?*

FOUR

THE ANIMALS MOVED THROUGH THE forest brush as easily as they moved through the darkness around them. Collin followed with considerable effort, tangling in briars and tripping over unseen branches. He could barely see them in the limited moonbeams jutting through the forest canopy. By the time he reached a mound of large rocks, they seemed to have completely disappeared.

They must have slipped between the gaps, he thought. He dropped to his knees on the forest floor. One by one, he strained to move the rocks to either side of him, creating a gorge in this miniature mountain.

Eventually, he unearthed a burrow in the ground, as tight and narrow as a coffin. He dismissed the thought of what animal so close to home could dig this human-sized hole and entered headfirst. With his arms outstretched in front of him and his stomach scraping along the ground, he slithered deeper into the earth, hoping he hadn't fallen too far behind the golden animals.

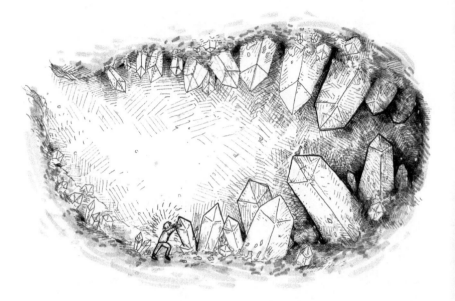

The tunnel turned from dirt to clay and from clay to stone. It became less and less constricting until he was no longer crawling but walking upright with the tunnel ceiling far above him. Out of the stone path broke jagged bursts of crystals, some small enough he could step over, some so large he had to climb. From the summit of the largest crystal, Collin finally caught another glimpse of the tiny animals and saw where they were going: everywhere around, above, and in front of them were various sizes of framed mirrors.

He watched the animals walk from the meandering crystal plateau toward a large reflective plane—just one of the thousands throwing their reflections. Without hesitation, each animal hopped over the base of the frame, passed through the mirror glass, and vanished.

Collin balanced himself at the edge of the frame and stepped forward, planting one foot flat in the unseen world on the other side of the mirror. The rest of his body teetered on the frame and was multiplied among the mirrored reflections. Countless Collins dipped their other foot into the mirror and immersed themselves into the unknown.

FIVE

THE REALM BEHIND THE MIRROR was dark and vast, and for the first time since waking, Collin was afraid. The room seemed to have no end in any direction. It was possible that it wasn't a room at all but a keyhole glance into a new universe that he gazed upon from one of its many edges.

The mirror portal he crossed through was now black above him. He stood on a small flat plane with nothing on it but the top of a ladder that rested against one edge. The other edges were drop-offs, the ground so far below him that it existed beyond his visual reach. The rest of the world was a nest of ladders—miles long and twisting—all leading to different portals. *Perhaps they lead to different parts of my world,* Collin thought. *Perhaps they lead to different worlds altogether.*

Collin spotted the golden animals already making their

way down the ladder. He lowered to his knees. One wrong move, and Collin knew this would be the end of his adventure. With one probing foot, he searched for where he needed to shift his weight in order to climb onto the ladder without incident.

He planted both feet on a rung near the top, and the rest of his body carefully moved into place. He began the downward climb behind the golden animals, the frame of the ladder bowing slightly with the addition of his weight. With alternating feet, he searched for the next rung below him. As he slunk down the ladder, Collin clung to the sides so tightly that his hands ached from strain.

It was then, while suspended and afraid, that he realized he wasn't alone. Hunched bodies crept up and down individual ladders all around him. Their eyes glistened red in the darkness. Sharp teeth protruded from their mouths, and their dark furry bodies moved as silently as stars. He couldn't tell if they noticed him or not, but he continued down the snaking ladder, shaking with every step.

SIX

AFTER WHAT FELT LIKE MILES OF descending, Collin made it to the last rung. Exhausted, his last step was more like a fall from the ladder, and a great *clang* came from his feet landing on the ground. The surface of this new world and every part of its scenery was made of rusting metal. Pipes coiled all around them like vines in a jungle. The golden animals strode forward like tiny sunspots in an eternity of corrosion.

"I know you're there. I've felt you following me," Collin whispered.

"Good instincts," the creature said. It crept down a pipe with such impossible physical ease that when their faces met, Collin was upright and the creature was upside down. Collin recognized its kind from the ladder world.

"What are you?" Collin asked.

"I'm from a species known as Realm Watchers." The creature's voice was a hiss that lingered in the air.

"You use the ladders?"

"Yes."

"To go where?" Collin asked.

"To go everywhere," it answered.

"Everywhere in the world?"

The creature paused for a moment and then said, "To go everywhere in your world and everywhere in all worlds and all the times in all the worlds that have been and will be too."

Collin's mind whirled trying to understand. Finally, he responded, "I'm human; my name's Collin."

"I already know you intimately well. I'm called Rorlitzer Screw."

Collin's eyes examined Rorlitzer Screw, and he noted that there was something eerily familiar about it, like reading your own name on a tombstone while walking through a graveyard.

"Better keep up with the Tinies, Collin." Rorlitzer Screw nodded toward the golden animals. "Not everyone who finds us is lucky enough to have protection."

SEVEN

A S THEY AMBLED THROUGH THE IN-
dustrial landscape, Collin noticed a stench beyond
the mineral smell of metal that he detected since his ar-
rival. The new smell was putrid and warm, like rotting
meat, and it became more pronounced the farther they
traveled. Little by little, the ground became littered with
bones; Collin had no choice but to feel their crunch beneath his feet.

Then he saw the two creatures responsible; identical
in appearance and humanoid in physique, they sat large
like mountains. Each head had a tangle of black hair that
shined wet with grease and hung down past its chest. Their
swelling bellies fell between their legs and suffocated the
floor. The skin across their stomachs stretched transparent
around their torsos and revealed a distorted window into
their gurgling digestive fluids and most recent appetites.

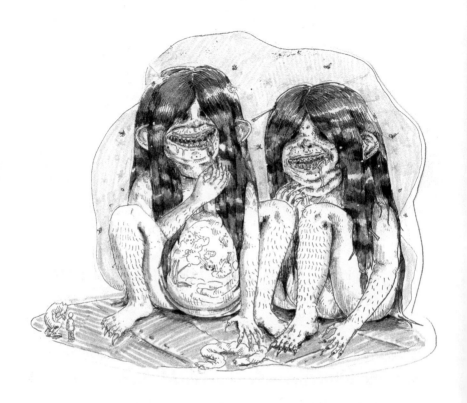

"And what is this now?" said one in a jovial, feminine
tone.

"A human?" said the other, matching her amusement.

"A boy!" they announced together.

The creatures peered through their hair to get a better
look. Collin stood arrested by fear.

"We do love boys around here, don't we, sister?"

"We do!"

"And it's so rare that we get company!"

"Very true, sister!"

"But why doesn't this one speak?" Silence engulfed the three of them while they awaited a response.

Collin finally squeaked, "Hello."

"See! That wasn't so hard!"

"Not hard at all! I'm Grylda."

"And I'm Zhar."

"We're twins, you know."

"Yes," Collin said. Uneasy, silent stares from the twins forced him to continue. His voice shook as he added, "It's nice to meet you."

The sisters erupted in a cackle of laughter.

"Is it now?" asked Grylda.

"Well, it definitely is for us," said Zhar, "but unless you like being eaten, I don't think it'll be nice for you at all." Zhar reached out with alarming speed and closed her giant hand around his body.

"Rorlitzer, help!" Collin screamed.

Grylda cackled again. "Rorlitzer Screw won't help you, boy."

Zhar joined in. "He'll only watch as we tear you apart!"

As both sisters held a part of Collin's squirming body in the air, a clamor came from a stack of nearby bones. They weren't alone, as the sisters had assumed.

In front of them, manifesting from the golden metal

seedling on the ground, grew a tiger as large and monstrous as the twins.

A growl revved in the tiger's throat as it readied to lunge. Its snarling mouth displayed golden, glistening rows of fangs. Its multiple pairs of eyes focused on attack—unblinking in concentration.

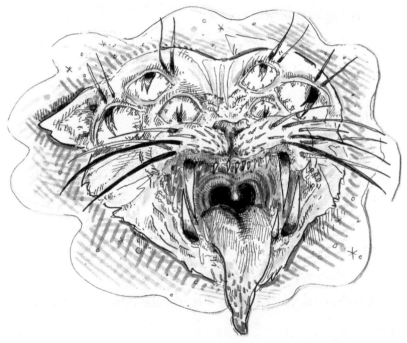

Grylda and Zhar responded with a cacophony of fearful shrieks and dropped Collin's body to the ground.

Collin scampered away from the twins. Once he was safe and out of their grasp, the giant tiger slowly shrank back down to its original size and form. They both joined the other Tinies waiting to continue their journey.

EIGHT

"YOU SAID YOU ALREADY KNEW ME," Collin said to Rorlitzer Screw. "What did you mean by that?"

"All Realm Watchers are assigned a human lineage beyond our world to watch. I've been assigned to your family for generations."

"So you watch over me?"

"I watch both you and your sister, yes, but I don't watch *over* you. I'm not there to offer protection." Rorlitzer Screw's voice was the sound of sand slithering across dried bones in a desert.

"That's what those creatures meant when I screamed for help," Collin said, to himself as much as to Rorlitzer Screw.

"Yes. As a species, we merely observe. We move in the shadows, and we watch events transpire. Our role is not an active one. It's almost unheard of for Realm Watchers and humans to have contact of any kind, and yet you are one of many from your father's bloodline who have found their way here and met me face-to-face."

"You met my father? He was here?" Collin's voice sped with interest.

"Yes, your father was here, and so was your grandmother, and your great-grandfather, and your great-great aunt, as far back as your history can trace."

"You met all of them? I didn't know so many people knew about this place!"

"Most people don't. But there's a strong curiosity in your family, as if you're more closely connected with realms that other humans aren't."

"That's awesome!" Collin yelled.

"Is it? That doesn't mean that being here isn't dangerous. I've watched many members of your family fall victim to creatures like the twins. There are monsters everywhere; it'll behoove you to remember that."

NINE

THE METAL LANDSCAPE SLOPED INTO the splashing edge of a vast sea. From where the tide licked the metallic coast to the distant horizon, all Collin saw was water. The Tinies weren't deterred and didn't hesitate submerging themselves. Collin waded into the water after them.

"How eagerly you follow," Rorlitzer Screw jeered. "You don't know what's in there. And I've seen you swim. You won't make it a mile."

"Well, I can't stop following them now." Collin's words broke as he attempted to keep his mouth above water. The waves slapped against him with such force that Collin was already struggling to stay afloat. His furious arm movements kept him from sinking, but even Collin realized he wouldn't be able to keep up the endurance or speed required for getting to wherever they were going. A realistic thought panicked him: *I'm going to drown here.*

He pushed that notion from his mind and fought against the current as hard as he could. Suddenly, something large and flat arose from the sea beneath him, lifting him up and out of the water. The surface was patterned in gold-tinged splotches. There were two stocky horns the same height as the boy. The golden giraffe was no longer tiny but stood as tall as the entire depth of the sea. Its hooves walked along the seabed as the top of its head bobbed above the water.

Collin was drenched and exhausted. His sweater, heavy from the weight of water-soaked fabric, showered his feet and the giraffe below him. His breathing slowed as he rested his back against one horn. Rorlitzer Screw perched atop the other.

"Kaitlin knows you're missing," Rorlitzer Screw said. "She's asleep, but in her dreams, she's looking for you."

"If she's asleep, how does she know I'm gone?"

"Children can feel beyond their present situation. They lose that gift with age, until they live like most other adults, rarely realizing there's anything more than what's right in front of them."

Collin understood. Though it wasn't concrete, hadn't he felt that change even as a child himself? Absolutes with no factual backing that had been *so real* to him years before he had already pushed aside as baby thoughts. He had intentionally moved away from imaginary friends. He had evicted the monster that lived in his closet.

Suddenly a thought crystallized in his mind, and he asked, "Will she remember our dad?"

"For a time, yes. Right now she's still able to interact with him as if he hasn't gone."

"What? How is that possible?"

"The boundary between his new world and hers is merely a fog. But as she gets older, that boundary will thicken, until full worlds separate them."

All around them swam monstrous life that Collin would never be aware of. Twisting leviathans and sharp-toothed blobs, tentacled echinoderms and spotted serpents all swirled between the surface of the water and the sand below.

"You were there at my father's accident," Collin realized.

"Yes, I was there and other places too," Rorlitzer Screw answered.

Collin's eyes swelled with tears that mingled with the ocean water trickling down his cheeks. "You were there, and you didn't stop it." His voice grew louder. "You watched it happen, and you didn't do anything."

"I can't interfere with your world ..."

"You mean you won't," Collin interrupted.

"Even if I wanted to, even if I tried to warn him in a dream, nothing would have changed."

"You don't know that!" He couldn't hold back his tears any longer and attempted to swat them away as they encroached.

"I know people, and they don't listen to dreams."

"But you said we were different! You said we were connected!" Collin shouted.

"As children, yes. But with age comes worry and justification. Open eyes become blindfolded, and adventure-seeking feet become entombed by cement." Rorlitzer Screw doubled in size as it returned Collin's hateful tone. "They drag along without question or knowledge of anything besides the constructs they've built for themselves: time and boundaries, what's real and imaginary, what's possible and impossible." With its teeth grimacing, it bellowed, "You forget your place, child! None of this is new! I've watched since your world's birth, and I'll watch until your world's fiery end!"

Rorlitzer Screw dove off the giraffe's horn into the water below. Collin traveled across the rest of the sea alone, but he knew Rorlitzer Screw was close. Its eyes were the water's reflection, its breathing the waves. Rorlitzer Screw was the sea, and Collin was a bug hoping for land.

Bernadine

Clara

Cecil

Kurt

Walter

Got lost in a shifting labyrinth of giant snakes and was left behind by her sister. Reported as a runaway. Was never seen again.

Assumed Bernadine for dead and hiked across the Inverted Mountains. Aged believing her sister ran away from home. Drowned herself in a river after giving birth to Kurt.

Humphry

Gertrude

Befriended a giant tortoise and rode it across 100 realms. Studied journalism in college. Traveled the world with Humphry before having Travis.

Travis

Frank

Kaitli

Joanne

Went on a quest with his dog Tip and the calcified creatures of the Volcano tribe.
Fell in love with Joanne in high school; worked to preserve the history of fading Indigenous cultures.

Set fire to an underground village of giant philosopher ants. Devoted his life to the Church; met Eloise in the choir.

= Siblings

= Offspring

= Spouses

Eloise

Claude

Bernard

A CURIOUS FAMILY TREE

Collin

Travels with a group of Tinies. May never return.

TEN

THE CELESTIAL CITY STOOD SOLItary on the other side of the sea. Towers with twisting steeples jutted up from the flat, gravelly sand that surrounded the city's perimeter. No buildings or life existed outside of the densely compacted cityscape chiseled by hand from master craftsmen out of huge pieces of lapis lazuli. The city was so named because of the deep-blue color of the mined stone and the golden speckles that naturally swirled throughout; looking at it was like staring into the cosmos, and being there was existing among stars. No one but the city's builders, aptly called the Celestials, lived there.

Rorlitzer Screw's footprints appeared in the sand before its body materialized next to Collin.

"It's incredible." Collin gazed upon the city as he and the Tinies followed the land path from the sea.

"That it is," said Rorlitzer Screw, "but be wary. The Celestials take great pride in their work. They don't like outsiders disturbing their progress."

"Progress? You mean it's still being built?"

"It's always being built. Inside, there are tunnels within tunnels and stairways within stairways all leading up and deeper within."

"Why don't they stop once it's finished?" Collin asked, his wide eyes following the subtle spiraling of the turrets.

"To the Celestials, it will never be complete. This is what they've always done, and this is what they'll always do. Their mining method is flawless; their chiseling technique is unmatched anywhere in the cosmos. They are born artisans, and they die virtuosos. This is their reason for living."

The Tinies led Collin and Rorlitzer Screw to an arched opening on the western side of the city. This part was engineered on both a horizontal grid and a vertical one. Surrounding buildings were linked together with large bridges at every story. From the ground looking up, walkable lattices spiraled upward, and everything was connected.

The use of vertical space created more room within this walled city, which meant even more possibility that Collin would get caught. He hunched low to the ground and hid in the shadows along the streets. He was careful to peek around corners before turning down the next alleyway. He always kept an eye up, just in case a Celestial may be on a bridge, watching him from above.

But each time the streets were empty. He hadn't seen any Celestials yet. The only indication that there was anyone else in the city besides Rorlitzer Screw, the Tinies, and himself was the unmistakable beauty of songs being played on a flute.

They followed the Tinies down another winding alley.

"Stay down." Rorlitzer Screw's voice had urgency in it, as if Collin were sticking his hand in an invisible flame.

"No one's even around," Collin said. They crossed through another courtyard and turned into another passageway.

"Don't be a fool! Can't you hear that?"

"The flutes? So what?"

"That's them!" Rorlitzer Screw snapped.

"Of course that's them. They must be practicing nearby." Collin gestured to the labyrinthine corridors that existed all around them.

"They're not practicing, human; they're communicating!" Rorlitzer Screw snarled. "And they're very close."

In that moment, three Celestials turned down the same alleyway, in direct view of Collin. The Celestials were short and angular, with few identifiable facial features: simple dark holes appeared to be their eyes; their mouths were slots forever open. They were each the same pale white, with pointed, stacked

winglets that fluttered from their sides. Their legs were unde-
fined—each torso its own thick stalk. They controlled the air
around them; instead of walking, they seemed to glide.

Face-to-face with Collin, they stopped moving. Their
jaws dropped—doubling the size of their heads—and each
began to screech in a high-pitched tone that
echoed through the corridors like
the sounding of an alarm.

The Tinies moved faster to the
dead end of the alley; Collin and
Rorlitzer Screw ran after them.
More Celestials gathered at the
entrance of the passageway,
quadrupling in number. The
Tinies finally reached a small
metal grate of ornate design
decorating the wall of the cul-de-
sac and leading outside the city.
The three of them moved quickly
through the bars. Rorlitzer Screw's
malleable body shrank and narrowed
to fit between the thin bars to join them.
Collin was trapped with nowhere to go.

"Please," Collin shouted desperately, "I'm looking for
an exit! I'm trying to leave!"

The Celestial mob moved toward him.

"I just want to go home!"

At that moment, the tiny golden rhino returned through the grate. It positioned itself beneath Collin and grew to a hulking size. With Collin sitting between its front shoulders and rear hump, it turned its massive golden body back around so that the grate was in front of them. The Celestials continued toward Collin, and when the rhino took steps backward to gather speed, they became that much nearer—the frenzied air from their bodies stinging Collin like static shock. The rhino shot into a straight gallop toward the lapis dead end. Collin shut his eyes and clung tightly to the rhino's back.

Huge cracks burst from the impact of the rhino's horn hitting the wall. The Celestials responded with deafening shrieks at the destruction of their work. The golden rhino charged again. Large chunks of lapis detached from the web of fractures covering the wall and smashed to the ground around them. It charged again and this time broke through the wall completely.

Beyond the city, only darkness existed. The rhino shrank to its original size and joined the Tinies leading the front of the pack. Behind them were strewn crumbles of the midnight lapis. A cloud of blue dust settled around the destruction. Instead of following them into the unknown, the Celestials began to clear away the rubble as the first step to restructuring their wall.

ELEVEN

THE FIVE OF THEM CREPT THROUGH blackness so dark that at first Collin lost all sight of his company. But the red gleam in Rorlitzer Screw's eyes began to glow in a way that lit the path and showed what was before them: a narrowing passageway that eventually scraped against the top of Collin's head so that he had to hunch down and slump over. It eventually became so tight that he was forced to crawl.

At the end of the passageway was a door, no bigger than the size of a cupboard. He gripped the knob and pulled it open. As Collin wiggled through the petite doorway, his eyes strained to adjust to the brightness of this new land.

It was huge and green and alive. Like an Earth jungle, trees grew large, with thick canopies of leaves overhead. Long, drooping vines connected trees together. The greenery was vibrant and varied. He was reminded of the lush woods he played in near his house during summertime, when the days stretched like words across a page and nighttime existed only as a footnote. Collin missed his home.

As he walked farther into the jungle, he noticed flits of movement all around him. Thousands of tiny golden animals peeked out from beneath leaves and scurried through patches of grass underfoot; some crossed vines like a tightrope, and those with wings darted through the air.

"What is this place?" Collin asked Rorlitzer Screw.

"This is the Valley of the Tinies," it said. "Your guides are finally home."

The tiger, the rhinoceros, and the giraffe escorted Collin and Rorlitzer Screw along a worn dirt path through the trees.

"I had no idea there were so many of them!"

"There are as many of them as there are stars in your sky," Rorlitzer Screw explained.

"Incredible."

"Just you wait."

The end of the path led to a massive cave that was still wholly cradled in the arms of the jungle. Despite two suns shining overhead, a drastic change in temperature emanated from the cold, damp rocks. Collin stopped walking and stared into the tremendous darkness in front of him.

"Do we have to go in there?" he asked.

"If you want to go home, this is the only way to do it."

From the darkness deep in the cave, a voice boomed, "Enter."

The volume and force of the voice surprised Collin so much that he began to tremble. The cave itself reverberated in response. "I have to go home," Collin whispered. With his heart racing, his steps were small and slow. He entered the darkness, his child frame swallowed by the mouth of the cave.

TWELVE

UPON ENTERING, COLLIN SAW THAT the cave was more illuminated than it had seemed from outside. Instead of the abyssal darkness he had expected, on either side of him, full-color projections beamed onto the walls of the cave. The projections were all in motion, like clips of movies playing next to each other. In front of each projection was an item on a stone pedestal, set so meticulously that it reminded Collin of museums on Earth. These odd couplings lined the walls of the corridor and continued deeper into the cave. There were hundreds of them.

"What is all of this?" Collin asked Rorlitzer Screw.

"You're in the home of the Gryphon King, ruler of the Tinies. Also known as the Collector of Memories. We're walking through his collection."

"Those are memories?" Collin nodded toward the walls.

"Yes." Rorlitzer Screw explained, "Each projection is a string of real memories given to the Gryphon King. Every projection is tied to the object in front of it. What you see are its associated memories."

"But where did they come from? Who did the objects belong to?" Collin asked.

"They all came from someone who—one way or another—found their way here."

"To this world? To this cave?"

"To this very spot. All of these objects were given as passage back to their world. The Gryphon King's payment."

Collin watched the collective movement on the walls, almost dizzying in its asynchrony. He began to understand. "So, I'll have to give him something, too, in order to get home?"

"Yes, but it can't be just anything. Like all of the items here, it has to have importance to the owner."

"But I don't have anything!" Collin's voice rose in panic. In a desperate act, he began to pat down his clothes, hoping to find something he had forgotten about. "I literally have nothing with me! How will I get home?"

"There is something you have," Rorlitzer Screw countered.

"What is it?" he asked.

"You have that sweater."

Taken aback, Collin stammered at the thought. "But ... but ... this isn't even *my* sweater. I can't just give it away."

"It doesn't matter who it belongs to, Collin. What matters are the memories that are given with it."

Collin shook his head. "I don't understand. What do you mean? The Gryphon King wants the memories too?"

"That's what all of this is." Rorlitzer Screw raised its clawed paw and motioned to the projections around them. "When someone gives away an object, they give away all memories of that object as well. They'll no longer be with you. They stay here with the Gryphon King."

Collin's eyes shined with tears. "But this was my father's. It was his favorite ..." His words trailed off.

"You wouldn't lose all memories of your father, just ones associated with the sweater."

Collin used the sleeve of his sweater to wipe the tears from his face. His tone was harsh and decided. "My father's dead. It's not like we're making new memories. I can't lose any of the ones I have of him. We have to find another way."

Rorlitzer Screw observed Collin's emotional display. "After all this time, you humans still surprise me. I'll talk to the Gryphon King and see if there's another option." It lowered to all fours.

"Wait," Collin said, "was my father here too?"

Rorlitzer Screw pointed farther down the corridor and then scurried with the speed of an exposed lizard as it left to find the Gryphon King.

THIRTEEN

COLLIN RECOGNIZED HIS FATHER'S face, as well as his uncle in the projections. Thinner, two feet shorter, and without the facial lines that come with age and understanding, a wiry ten-year-old Frank flashed on the wall. The object on the pillar was a piece of rope tied into a loop on one end. Like watching strung-together clips of home recordings, Collin sat down on the cool cave floor. Through crying eyes, he studied his father's missing childhood memories.

MEMORY 1

Two boys are playing in front of a house when they hear a growling from behind the bushes on the edge of the yard. "It's getting dark, anyway. We need to get inside," the older says. "You're such a chicken," Frank says. "We'll see what Mom has to say about that," the older says as he runs back to the house. Frank steps slowly in the direction of the growling.

MEMORY 2
Behind the bushes is a white dog with a black-tipped tail. Its lips are pulled back, displaying sharp teeth, its front paws batting at a snake curled on the ground. "Hey there, boy," Frank says, "it's just a rat snake. He's not a bad guy. Come over here. You want some?" Frank pulls out a piece of jerky from his pocket. The dog follows the scent, and while it eats from Frank's hand, the rat snake slithers away. "Good boy. How do you like the name Tip?"

MEMORY 3
Frank brings bowls from the kitchen and sets them on the front porch. He shouts, "Dinnertime!"

MEMORY 4
A sunny day. Frank plays chase with Tip in the yard.

MEMORY 5
On the front porch, Frank sneaks meat from a napkin in his pocket. "At least one of us likes fried liver."

MEMORY 6

Frank talks to his father in the living room. "But why can't he come in the house?" Frank asks. "He's just a neighborhood mutt, Frankie. He'll be okay outside; he likes it there."

MEMORY 7

Frank steps onto the porch in his pajamas at night. No lights are on inside the house. "Did you see that, boy?" A shadow falls from the tree and glides across the yard. "Come on! Let's follow it!" Frank grabs a rope from the shed and loops it around Tip's neck. "Just in case. I don't want you running away and getting hurt." They move through the darkness, starting their adventure together.

The flashes replayed in an unending loop. Instead of watching them for a tenth time, Collin stood up and saw Rorlitzer Screw standing behind him.

"He couldn't just leave the rope, since it wasn't important to him." Collin's eyes were red, cheeks wet from tears. His tone was cold and matter-of-fact. "So you made him leave his dog."

"You're right about the rope. But I didn't make him do anything. I told him the requirements for leaving, just as I've told you. If you want to blame somebody for your father's missing memories, blame that Giant Mountain Midge he followed here. Or blame him for going on such a foolhardy quest."

"Shut up!" Collin exploded. "Just shut up for once! It's never your fault, right? Everyone else is to blame, but never you!"

"I merely ..."

"Observe? Yeah, I know, I know! You just sit there and watch it all crumble around you. And that's great for you and the rest of your kind, but when anybody needs any actual help, you just disappear! You may as well be a clock or a chair or a clump of dust. So what if people die? So what if memories get taken? At least you can feel good knowing that you watched the whole thing fall apart. And a boy grows up without his dog, and children grow up without a father, but that's okay, cause you were there observing every second of it!"

Rorlitzer Screw stayed silent, but a voice arose from deep in the cave. "It's not Rorlitzer Screw's fault that he's following orders, Collin. But I like your spirit. It's nice to make your acquaintance. I'm the Gryphon King."

FOURTEEN

FROM THE DAMP GROUND TO THE budding stalactites on the ceiling, the Gryphon King's huge lion body filled the empty vertical space of the cave. Its wings were tucked at either side, leaving the reality of its massive wingspan to Collin's imagination. Similar to the golden Tinies that it reigned over, the Gryphon King was completely gold in color, its feathers and fur twinkling in the darkness of the cave.

"Rorlitzer Screw has expressed your desire to return home, as well as your concern about leaving your father's sweater. There is one other option that I think you'd be interested in."

"Yes, sir. I am interested! Anything!"

"It would call for a duel—a fight between you and an opponent of my choosing. And you would have to win."

"A fight? But I don't know how to fight." He then spoke

a crushing fact that reminded Collin just how helpless he actually was. "I'm only eleven years old." He pleaded, "Is there no other way?"

"Going home requires some amount of sacrifice, Collin. This can be in the form of objects and memories or through a physical gamble that could result in you staying here forever. These are your options."

"Your Highness," Rorlitzer Screw began, "might the boy and I have some time to mull this over together? I think ..."

"No," Collin interrupted, "I'll fight. I'll do it. I have to."

"Very well, Collin," the Gryphon King said.

"The boy doesn't understand, Your Highness. He doesn't realize ..."

"His mind is made up, Rorlitzer Screw. And I'll remind you that the decision is wholly his to make."

Rorlitzer Screw swallowed the rest of its sentence and forced its mind down a different route. "Will you tell us what he'll be fighting, Your Majesty?"

"He'll be fighting a Flecian. You may both stay the night in my kingdom. The battle will commence at dawn."

FIFTEEN

THE SUNS WERE SETTING WHEN Rorlitzer Screw and Collin walked out of the Cave of Memories and back into the jungle. The two of them sat on soft ground covered in leaves and ate fruit collected for them by the Tinies.

"I know what you're thinking," Collin said between bites of a seedy pink fruit that seemed the otherworldly cousin of a cantaloupe.

"And what's that?" Rorlitzer Screw asked.

"You're thinking how stupid I am. Maybe even how stupid all humans are."

"No, I was thinking how reckless you are but also how brave. I've never known any Realm Watcher to put its life on the line for anything."

In that moment, Collin was proud of his decision. Maybe this was a human attribute that no other species in all the worlds had: a willingness to lose everything for something they cared about—even something intangible like memories.

"Do you know what the Gryphon King did with my father's dog once he went home?" Collin asked. "I hope it wasn't left to die in a cage somewhere in his collection."

"The Gryphon King is an avid collector, but he's also the ruler over an entire land of animals. He wouldn't want it to suffer like that. The dog has made a home somewhere beyond the jungle now."

"Now? You mean it's still alive? That's impossible, it must have been …"

"Thirty-two years ago."

"Right! Dogs don't live that long."

"On Earth," Rorlitzer Screw corrected. "But this place has a way of changing things. Animals can live a long time here." It paused and then added, "You have noticed a few differences between your world and ours, haven't you?"

Collin stared at Rorlitzer Screw and then laughed for the first time since arriving. "I think that's the first joke I've heard you make!"

"It doesn't happen very often." With its sharp teeth, Rorlitzer Screw tore through the flesh of the purple fruit nestled in its paws. Juice dripped from its mouth and fingers as it gnawed, creating an unexpectedly gory scene. Collin thought again about the battle.

"What's a Flecian?"

Rorlitzer Screw finished eating and tossed the core of the fruit into the trees behind them.

"A Flecian is a large biped from the Grasslands. Since it's fighting for the Gryphon King, we can assume it's from the warrior clan, thus very strong and capable in battle. Their whole bodies are covered in tangled fur so thick it acts as natural armor, and they have forward-facing horns like those of rams on Earth."

"Will I be able to beat it?"

"No."

There has to be a way, he thought to himself. He searched his mind, thinking of any scenario that would render him victorious the next day. Then he asked, "Do they have any weaknesses I could aim for? That happens in video games all the time!"

Rorlitzer Screw thought for a moment and then said, "Swamp Worms' hearts grow outside of their skin."

"Right, like that!"

"But only the external five hearts are like that. They still have at least one internal heart that can keep them alive."

"Oh."

"There is also an entire living island that will sink into the ocean if a single specific flower is plucked. But which flower is a heavily guarded secret." Rorlitzer Screw thought for a moment longer and then said, "No, Flecians don't have anything of that sort. I've known some that are less intelligent than others, but that's the same with everything. Except Muter Minds. That species is all genius."

Collin sighed. "It was just a thought, anyway."

"I have heard a legend from the Glasslands. It's of a giant beast that lives in isolation on the volcanic western edge. They say it's the last of its kind. Flecians use it as a threat with their young to scare them into behaving and as a challenge to their warriors to test their courage. But none have actually seen it, or if they have, they haven't lived to tell about it. It's merely a tall tale, as Earthlings say."

Darkness crept in, and they sat in silence. Collin finally asked, "What happens if I lose?"

"Then you stay here forever," Rorlitzer Screw responded.

Collin suspected that might be the case and asked, "What would happen back home?"

"They'd be devastated. They'd assume you ran away, and they'd search for you everywhere they could. There would be no closure. Your mother would live the rest of her life expecting to see you again."

Tears slid down Collin's cheeks at the thought of hurting his mother like that. "What's Mom doing now?"

Rorlitzer Screw's eyes peered through the impervious fog veil that only it could see and said, "She's dreaming about your father." Collin found comfort in that, if even the slightest amount.

"You've had a long day. You should try to get some sleep." Rorlitzer Screw crawled up a tree, leaving Collin stretched out on the jungle floor. They listened to the calls of the nighttime Tinies, and Collin finally shut his eyes for the first time since waking in his bedroom. Back before he knew anything else existed besides family and school. Back when he had only walked the land of one world. Back a lifetime ago.

SIXTEEN

NIGHT PASSED QUICKLY. COLLIN couldn't tell if it was a characteristic of this world or if he was so nervous about his upcoming battle that darkness vanished before he could reach that deepest layer of sleep. But now he was wide awake in the fading shadows before dawn. And he was afraid.

"Here," Rorlitzer Screw said, "you will need a weapon. I made this for you while you slept." It handed Collin a long, sturdy stick that was sharpened to a point on one end.

"Thank you," Collin said and felt the weight of the makeshift spear in his hands. He knew he would have to use all his strength to thrust the pointed edge into whatever vulnerable meat he could find on the Flecian.

While the suns rose, he and Rorlitzer Screw stood together and waited at the mouth of the cave in silence. A refrain played in his mind: *This is how I see my family again; this is what I have to do to get home.*

The Gryphon King walked out of the cave and spread its incredible wings. It pushed downward with so much force that its body was thrust straight into the air and landed on top of the cave above them. There it perched as spectator to the upcoming duel on the ground below. Rorlitzer Screw moved toward the edge of the forest line, making sure to provide plenty of open space.

And then Collin saw it: the massive shape lumbering toward him out of the mouth of the cave was his opponent. It towered over him. There was nothing lean about its frame; its body was thick with muscle. Protective, densely matted fur existed everywhere except its horns and head. Its face was scarred, proving a lifetime of battle wins.

The Gryphon King commanded the fight to begin.

At once, the Flecian dropped to all fours and ran—horns first—toward Collin. Everything inside of Collin wanted to run, but he knew he couldn't. This was his way home. As the Flecian galloped toward him, he stood his ground. He put all his weight behind holding his spear sturdy. He aimed for the fast-approaching skull. He shut his eyes.

The collision was enough to knock Collin to the ground. The shock of the blow rattled him, but as far as he could tell, he wasn't hurt. Because the spear hit first, Collin's small body wasn't trampled by this animal with the force of a freight train but was merely pushed to the side.

The Flecian didn't react from the jab of the spear. It slowed itself enough to turn around and headed back toward Collin at full speed. Collin clambered to his feet and once again held the spear in front of him, pointed directly at the oncoming skull. But this time, just before the Flecian met the weapon, it whipped its head to the side and used its impressive horns to obliterate Collin's spear. The point exploded. What used to be a spur carved by the claws of Rorlitzer Screw became first a puff of splintering wood and second the flattened nub end of a stick. The shaft of the spear split in half. Again, Collin was knocked to the ground. But this time when he got up, he was dizzy from the blow and bewildered by the dulled, broken stick he now wielded for protection.

Before Collin regained his bearings, the Flecian charged again and hit him squarely in the stomach. His body was thrown near the tree line and landed with a thud in the dirt. He would have cried out in pain if the air hadn't been knocked out of him. Instead, he lay on the ground holding his stomach. His sweater clung to him in tatters; two long rips now existed down the front from the force of the Flecian's horns. Tears flowed down Collin's cheeks as he gasped for breath.

From the sidelines of the fight, Rorlitzer Screw emitted a beckoning whistle as loud as an alarm. The Flecian circled back around to run toward Collin again, but this time it hesitated. As it stared into the trees past Collin's deflated body, something large was responding to Rorlitzer Screw's whistle. It was fast approaching and rustling the jungle as it neared. A deep, low growl moved through the trees. Before the Flecian had time to react, a large animal sprang from the jungle and landed in front of Collin.

Its body was white. The many golden eyes on its enormous head flashed with violent fervency. Its mouth snarled with fangs. Unlike the Flecian that walked on two legs but ran its fastest on all four, it was clear that this animal never knew life on two legs. But it was fast and strong. It pounced from its hind legs and collided with the Flecian. Numerous claws dug into the fur of the Flecian's chest. Controllable tendrils snaked out of its body and pulled the Flecian to the jungle floor.

As the large animals wrestled each other on the ground, a mushroom cloud of dirt rose above the carnage. There was a ferociousness in the animal that frightened Collin, but as he remained on the ground struggling to breathe, he also thought that it seemed somehow familiar. *Was the tip of its tail a flash of black?* This was his last thought as unconsciousness swept over him and forced him into darkness.

SEVENTEEN

COLLIN OPENED HIS EYES AS IF AWAKening from a deep sleep. To his surprise, it was nighttime, and he was lying in his own bed. His body was sore, and pain shot through his abs as he tried to sit up. He remembered the fight; the tatters of his father's sweater loosely draped around him acted as evidence. In truth, it was hardly a sweater at all anymore. He fought for these threads, but more importantly, he fought for the memory of his father.

He recalled everything from his adventure, starting with leaving his room and traveling through different worlds with his golden companions. He glanced at the now empty box they originated from on his bedside table. *They made it home*, he thought to himself, *and because of Rorlitzer Screw, I made it home.* Safe and exhausted, he closed his eyes and fell back asleep.

Rorlitzer Screw and Tip, the once forgotten dog, walked side by side in the jungle.

"That was nice what you did for the boy." The dog's voice was a husky whisper.

"You did the fighting; that's what saved him," Rorlitzer Screw responded.

"Yeah, but you're the one that broke the rules." Golden Tinies speckled underfoot and flitted through the greenery above them. "So what happens now?"

"Now they come," Rorlitzer Screw said, "but first they have to find me."